# Paul Bun

## A Tall Ta

retold by Laura Layton Strom

illustrated by Jack Snider

More than 100 years ago,
a very big baby was born.
His name was Paul Bunyan.
He was the biggest baby ever seen.

It took five storks to carry
him to his mom and dad!

Paul grew very fast. His pants became shorts. *SHRINK!*

His shirt split in two. *RIP!!*

He gained *eighty* pounds each day!

At age one week, he was as big as his dad.

He wore his dad's clothes.

Baby Paul liked to eat. If he got too hungry, his tummy rumbled. The rumbles caused earthquakes.

Baby Paul ate more than forty bowls of hot cereal every morning. *SLURP!* That was his morning snack. Then he ate his real breakfast.

RUMBLE

Paul's lungs were mighty strong. He had quite a cry. He could empty a pond with one loud *WHAAA*! Frogs and fish went flying.

Paul grew bigger and bigger every day. Soon he was all grown up. He was more than thirty feet tall.

His dad's clothes did not fit anymore.
The whole town came together to sew.
They made shirts and pants for Paul.
They used wagon wheels for his buttons.

Paul needed a job. He loved to chop
and cut wood. So he became a logger.

Paul cut faster than anyone.
He cut down 1,000 trees every day.

Wood piled up to the moon.

Paul liked to eat before he worked. He liked pancakes the most. It took more than fifty men to make pancakes for Paul.

Paul ate pounds and pounds of pancakes.

SYRUP

One day the men were busy. They could not make pancakes for Paul. Paul grew sad. He walked away with his big ax dragging behind him.

The ax cut a big hole in the ground. The hole was one mile deep. It was 277 miles long. Today that hole is called the Grand Canyon.